The Adventures of the Owl and the Pussycat

written by Coral Rumble

illustrated by Charlotte Cooke

PaRragon

Bath · New York · Cologne · Melbourne · Delhi
Hong Kong · Shenzhen · Singapore · Amsterdam

The Owl and the Pussycat went to sea
In a box on the living room floor.
They sailed away for a year and a day,
And these are the things that they saw …

A wiggly, squiggly eel
Dancing with a cheerful seal,

A bottle bobbing by
With a treasure map inside,

A shark in a spin
With a cat on his fin,

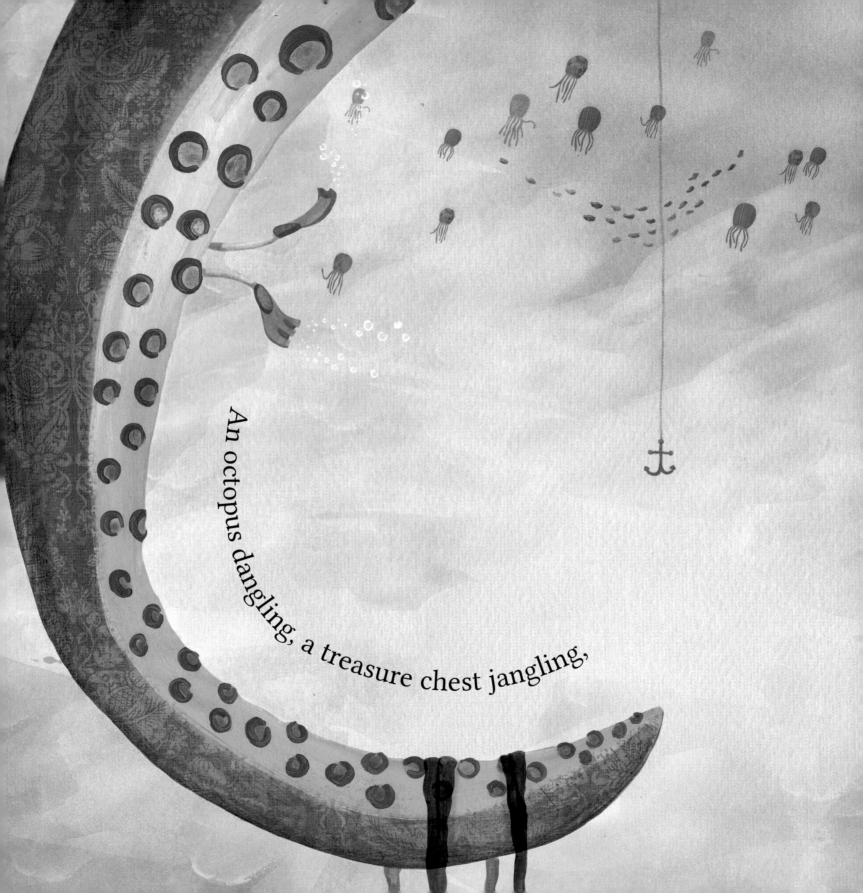

An octopus dangling, a treasure chest jangling,

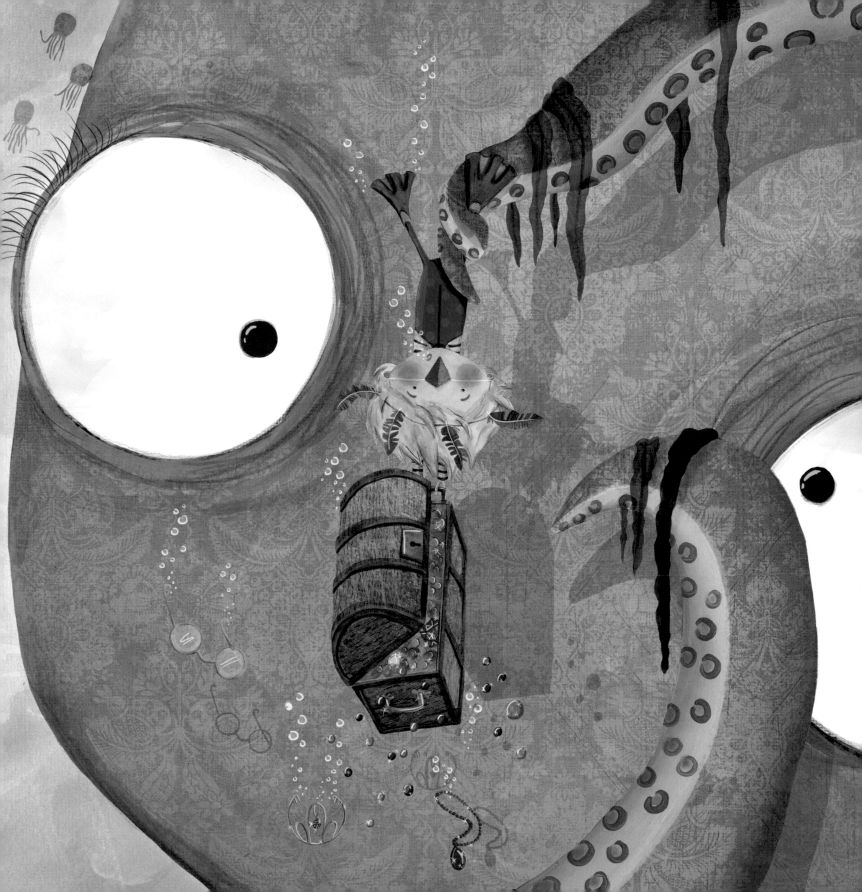

A clownfish playing the flute

In a bow tie and a suit,

A starfish in the sun,

A naughty seagull
having fun,

A lobster playing catch

With a crab who likes to snatch,

A swordfish in a fight
With a pirate late at night,

A puffin in a cap flying around the moon and back,

A cave on the shore
With a green seaweed door ...

The Owl and the Pussycat went to sea
In a box without very much room.
Then hand in hand they sailed back to land,
And slept by the light of the moon,
The moon, the moon ...

And slept by the light of the moon.

For Andy, the BUMP & Amelia;
my very own naughty Seagull.
C.C.

For Jean & Gordon,
(my PARENTS).
C.R.

This edition published by Parragon Books Ltd in 2014 and distributed by

Parragon Inc.
440 Park Avenue South, 13th Floor
New York, NY 10016

www.parragon.com

Published by arrangement with Gullane Children's Books

Text © Coral Rumble 2013
Illustrations © Charlotte Cooke 2013

ISBN 978-1-4723-4604-9

Printed in China